First published 2019 by Walker Books Ltd
87 Vauxhall Walk, London SE11 5HJ

2 4 6 8 10 9 7 5 3 1

This book has been typeset in Sabon

Printed in China

British Library Cataloguing in Publication Data:
a catalogue record for this book is
available from the British Library

ISBN 978-1-4063-8592-2

www.walker.co.uk

FATHER'S DAY

Shirley Hughes

WALKER BOOKS
AND SUBSIDIARIES
LONDON · BOSTON · SYDNEY · AUCKLAND

I love spending time
with my dad.

Sometimes Olly and I jump
on Dad to wake him up
in the morning...

And sing to him
while he eats
his breakfast.

I chat to Dad
when he takes me
to playgroup…

When we walk
along the street...

And when we're
in the car.

Today is a special day.

We go to the beach
and set up a perfect
spot to play.

We make a sandcastle
together…

And sit down to
have some lunch.

When we get home,
I help Dad give
Buster a bath.

I try to give the cat
a bath too, but she
scratches me.

So Dad gives my
poor arm a kiss
and a plaster.

Then Dad gives
us a bath!

At bedtime,
Dad tells me
a story...

And shows me
the moon behind
the clouds.

I love spending
time with my dad.